For my sisters & brothers across the sea: Precious and Michael Afolayan,
Yvette Houngbo, Rebecca Mbuh, Eve Thompson, Senyo Opong, Frances Igboeli, and Mengistu Abate.
For my sister, Debora Johnson-Ross, citizen of America, daughter of Africa.
For Valerie A. Smith, Charleston sister, cherished mentor.
For the brilliant and beautiful Brook Lynn & Hope Imani Stewart.
For my great-nieces, Zoe Soleil & Aria Shay Johnson, amazing in every way.

—D.J.

Indigo Dreaming

Text copyright © 2022 by Dinah Johnson

Illustrations copyright © 2022 by Anna Cunha

All rights reserved. Manufactured in Italy.

No part of this book may be used or reproduced in any manner whatsoever without written permission except in the case
of brief quotations embodied in critical articles and reviews. For information address HarperCollins Children's Books,
a division of HarperCollins Publishers, 195 Broadway, New York, NY 10007.

www.harpercollinschildrens.com

Library of Congress Control Number: 2021949282

ISBN 978-0-06-308020-1

Typography by Dana Fritts

22 23 24 25 26   RTLO   10 9 8 7 6 5 4 3 2 1

❖

First Edition

Indigo dreaming

written by
Dinah Johnson

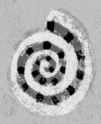

illustrated by
Anna Cunha

HARPER
An Imprint of HarperCollinsPublishers

Every morning at day-clean,
when the sun is just about to rise,
I pretend that Indigo Beach is mine!

And every morning at day-clean,
I wonder if somewhere there's a girl like me,

who spends every day beside the sea.

Does she squirm while her mama braids her hair?
Does she pick out an indigo dress to wear?

Does she run, like I do, slicing the air
like a bird's wings on the wind,
leaving the shapes of her feet in the sand?

I wonder if somewhere in the world
there's another busy girl,
searching for sweetgrass to make a basket.

Or is she combing the beach for pretty shells?
Does she know that if she holds them up to her ear,
she will hear the ocean sing its song
in Barbados, Brazil, or Sierra Leone?

Is there a girl across the sea who imagines me?

I stand still just long enough
to get a treat from my pocket,
and I wonder if there's a girl
on the other side of the world
eating scrumptious boiled peanuts too—

Does she call them goobers like I do?
Does she lick the juice running down her chin?

I wonder if there's a girl like me
across an ocean or a sea,
playing on a beach like Indigo Beach,
in the waves with dolphin and fish—
splash into the water and make a wish!

I close my eyes and imagine a girl
in some other faraway part of the world,

who plays in a circle with her friends—
now she's out and now she's in.

Then crack!
The thunder is loud—like a handclap game.

I stick out my tongue for a taste of rain.
Is that girl doing the very same thing?

Maybe she's running as fast as I am,
her footprints disappearing in the shimmering sand,
darting from palm tree to swooshing palm,
zigzagging like a crab all the way back home.

We're eating Frogmore Stew tonight.
Would that girl, far away, like to have a bite?

I wonder if that girl across the sea
likes coconut water or sweet iced tea?

Does her grandma, like mine, sit close beside her,
telling bedtime stories about Anansi the Spider?

Is that girl counting every star?
In the indigo sky, they don't seem so far
away . . .

Karimba music is in the air.
Can *that* girl hear it over there?
Is she falling asleep to its quiet beat?

I think we're looking at the very same moon
as its glowing fills both our rooms.

In my heart,
I'm *sure* there's another girl like me
across an ocean or a sea,
spending the night in an indigo dream

of the two of us playing
in the same sun,
in the same sand,
hand in hand—
every morning at day-clean.

A Note from the Author

The African Americans who live on the South Carolina, Georgia, and Florida Sea Islands are the descendants of the enslaved people who were taken largely from the country of Sierra Leone on the west coast of the African continent. These Africans in America are called the Gullah or the Geechee people. They have a unique culture and a distinct language that developed because of their isolation. For example, the word *goober* means "peanut." And the term *day-clean* means "dawn"—that time when the day is brand-new.

Fortunately, the Gullah people have reconnected with their African family across the sea. In 1988 a former president of Sierra Leone, Joseph Saidu Momoh, visited the Gullah community of St. Helena Island, South Carolina, and a group of Gullah people visited Sierra Leone in 1989. You can learn about this by watching the documentary film *Family Across the Sea* and its sequel, *Gullah Roots*. Together, these communities in the United States and Sierra Leone have discovered all that they still share—not only language, but ways of making baskets, fishing, naming their children, worshipping, experiencing time, and seeing their world. All over the African Diaspora, people tell stories about characters like Anansi the Spider and Br'er Rabbit.

Another thing they have in common is indigo. Africans on the Continent, on the Sea Islands of South Carolina, and in the Brazilian region of Bahia are experts in producing indigo dye to create a breathtakingly beautiful shade of blue used for fabric.

I hope that *Indigo Dreaming* inspires you to learn about people on the coast of Africa or North or South America or in other parts of the world whose lives might be a lot like yours in big or little ways. And maybe in the future, you will visit some of these places and not just imagine the people—but meet them!

I am a child of South Carolina, born in Charleston, not far from the Sea Islands. And I treasure my trips to Africa. *Indigo Dreaming* is inspired by my love for these special places. But my story is not meant to be a faithful, factual representation of any real communities. It is my love song to the Sea Islands, to my African friends, and to all I am blessed to count as family, at home and across the sea.